A HOT JOCKS NOVELLA

# THE BEDROOM EXPERIMENT

*New York Times* & *USA Today* Bestselling Author

# KENDALL RYAN

# ABOUT THE BOOK

Determined college co-ed Isla uses her spring break to conduct a little experiment...a bedroom experiment. Living under the same roof for the first time since their parents married, hot-as-heck hockey player Morgan doesn't know it yet, but he's about to become her test subject.

*This is a hot and steamy, low-drama standalone novelette. Contents include: One sweet but rough around the edges hockey player who's going a little crazy. One blunt, knows-what-she-wants heroine who picks through his self-defense. No cheating. No angst. No stress. And a sweet, melty HEA.*

# CHAPTER ONE

*Morgan*

"Can you pass me a slice of mushroom?" Isla asks from the other side of the counter.

I open the box and place a slice of pizza onto the plate she's holding out, crinkling my nose at the noxious fungi she insisted on ordering.

I was twenty and away at college when our parents married, and Isla moved into my childhood home. She was seventeen, nerdy, and obsessed with that young adult vampire book series that was popular at the time. It was oddly adorable. I saw her occasionally, during Christmas and spring break, but it was when I moved home for the summer that everything started to change. Isla started to change.

She replaced her glasses with contacts, grew a set of tits, and ditched the braces. Oh, and let's not forget her newfound fondness for wearing short as fuck shorts. She was a good girl. Smart as hell, a star on the tennis team, head of the student council, and focused on a crazy amount of time on extracurriculars to ensure she got into the best college.

I immediately started limiting my time at home, because Isla was jail bait—more attractive than she should have been, and completely off-limits to me, her brand-spanking-new stepbrother.

But now I have no choice but to be at home. Our parents, both oncologists at the same busy hospital, are finally taking a delayed honeymoon to Hawaii, two and a half years after their wedding. And it's why I knew I couldn't put up a fight when they asked me to spend this weekend with Isla during her winter break from her sophomore year of college. I'm supposed to be looking after her.

I keep telling myself it's fine, that I'll be fine being around her on our own. I'm twenty-two years old now, not some hormonal teenager who can't keep his dick in his pants. Plus, she's still my goddamn step sister.

Isla takes a healthy bite of her pizza, flashing me a look as she chews. "Mushrooms are awesome."

I shrug. "The psychedelic kind aren't so bad."

Her inquisitive blue eyes widen. "You've done that? And yet you won't even let me have a drink?"

"Actually no, I haven't. It was a joke." Some friends of mine had, but I'd always been more focused on sports and had little time for things that distracted me from that. "Tell me, why do you want a drink so bad?"

Isla shrugs. "I drink at college sometimes, you know."

I bring my bottle of beer to my lips and take a long swig. "I'm sure you do."

She rolls her eyes, finishing the last of her pizza, and then carries her plate over to the sink. I watch her ass as she rinses the plate and places it in the dishwasher.

Forcing myself to turn away, I polish off my beer and head to the fridge for another.

"So, what are we going to do tonight?" she asks as she wipes down the marble countertops and puts the rest of the pizza away. "We could watch a movie."

I nod. "If you want." This might be the house I grew up in, but since Isla and her mom moved in, there's been a lot of upgrades. Including my old bedroom, that's now a media room, complete with surround sound and a movie screen-style projector. I didn't really imagine that Isla and I would *hang out* while I was here. I figured she'd be busy with her friends, or maybe catching up on studying.

She grins and her eyes twinkle. "Cool. I'm just going to go call Tyler, and then I'll come find you."

Tyler's her boyfriend. I haven't met the guy, but she talks about him enough that I swear I've met him a million times before. I know he's a political science major and two years ahead of her in school. They met her first week on campus and have been dating all year. She's been talking about him almost nonstop for the past two days. Tyler this. Tyler that. I'm not annoyed by that at all.

With a sigh, I take my bottle of beer and head into the media room, deciding to look through the movie selection while I wait for Isla to finish her phone call.

Almost an hour slides by as I nurse my beer and dick around on my phone. A couple of my teammates are going out to a bar we like back home. I live a couple of hours away and just got drafted to

Seattle's pro hockey team as a backup goalie. It's an amazing opportunity, and one I take very seriously.

My phone rings and it's Owen, the team's star goalie and one of my personal idols.

"Hey dude," I say when I answer. "What's up?"

"Come out with us, bro."

"We need Morgan," I hear someone say in the background. I think it's Landon. "The pickup game is strong in that one."

He isn't wrong. I'd finally grown into my frame these last couple of years. When I hit six foot four my freshman year of college, my dad wondered if I'd ever stop growing. He's only average height so my growth spurt was unexpected. I'd been lanky and thin until I finally put on thirty pounds of muscle. That, coupled with the new edition of my half-sleeve of ink, the guys on my team loved to tease me that I was a pussy magnet. I gotta admit, I didn't hate their new nickname.

"You down or what?" Owen asks.

"Can't. I'm at my dad's house this weekend, two hours away."

"Twat?" he says. "I cunt hear you?" I chuckle,

but Owen's not done. "I think I have an ear in-fuck-tion. Don't worry, I'll finger it out."

I laugh again. As the rookie on the team, it's practically their job to give me shit. "Have fun tonight guys."

After promising to go out with them when I return, I end the call.

I check my watch, and decide rather than wait around for Isla, I'm going to hit the hot tub. I grab my navy-blue board shorts from my duffel bag and change quickly. My muscles are sore from last week's game, and as I ease down into the hot, bubbling water, I let out a low hiss hoping the heat will relieve some of the tightness.

It would have been nice to go out with the guys tonight, rather than being stuck here babysitting, but what can you do? Leaning my head back against the edge of the hot tub, I look up at the cloudless night sky. The stars are brighter here somehow, and I take a moment to appreciate the view.

The silence is interrupted by the sound of the back door opening. I watch Isla pad out across the travertine walkway in bare feet. Her face is red, and her eyelashes are damp with tears.

I straighten up and face her. "What's wrong?"

She shakes her head, her long dark hair falling over one cheek. "I don't want to talk about it." Her voice is a little hoarse.

"Are you okay?" I ask. I grew up as an only child, just me and my dad, and have next to no experience with crying females so I'm fumbling through motions and thinking back to what I've seen guys do in movies and television shows when faced with this exact situation.

She shakes her head and I watch a single tear roll down over her cheek.

*Fuck.*

"Is it something with Tyler?"

She bites her lip, looking down into the bubbling water. "Tyler who?"

Well, I guess that answers that. Against my better judgment, I slide over on the bench, and gesture to her. "Get your suit on. Come get in."

Thinking it over for a moment with a contemplative look, she nods once, and disappears back into the house.

A minute later, she's back and dressed in a skimpy white bikini that looks amazing against her honey-colored skin. She's carrying two bottles of beer. She hands them to me, then slips in beside me.

Isla makes a small noise of pleasure as she sinks into the water.

I open the first beer, and hand it to her. Even if part of me doesn't like the idea of her drinking, I know one beer won't hurt anything—and she might need it if she really did just break up with her boyfriend.

"Thanks," she says, voice soft.

She brings the bottle to her lips, and they press together, the delicate column of her throat working as she swallows.

I clear my throat and avert my eyes as she leans back, exposing the tops of her luscious breasts that spill over the top of the bikini.

Jesus Christ. This was not my best idea.

I open the second bottle and take a long drink, trying to quench the sudden thirst I have.

"Want to talk about it?" I ask, digging myself even deeper.

I kind of hope she doesn't, but I'm trying to be the grown-up in this situation.

"Tyler broke up with me," she says before taking another small sip of her beer.

*Shit.* I'm not equipped to handle teenage drama. Granted, she's only a few of years younger than me, but still, I'm not equipped, and I really don't want to handle this.

"I'm sorry," I say, before taking another large gulp of beer while simultaneously wishing it was something stronger.

Isla waves me off. "He said I wasn't *experienced* enough." She makes air quotes as she says this, scoffing like she's annoyed.

Okay, not the conversation I wanted to be having with her tonight, let alone ever, and sure as hell not when she's sitting next to me practically naked, but fuck it. The least I can do is listen. Maybe try to offer a little advice. "So, what happened?" I ask, diving right in.

"I was going to go all the way with him on Valentine's Day and give him my V-card on V-day. I thought that'd be romantic."

I almost choke on the beer in my throat. Valentine's Day is next weekend, and I do not like the idea of her giving it away to some undeserving prick. Recovering, I cough once into my fist and then look over at Isla. "I guess you dodged a bullet then."

She looks at me like I've sprouted a second head. "Not hardly. If I want to be able to keep a boyfriend, I obviously need more experience in the bedroom, *not less*."

I turn to face her. "This guy is obviously a tool, Isla. Anyone who tells you that you're not good enough or experienced enough isn't someone you want to be with. Any guy would be lucky to have you."

Her lips twitch with the hint of a smile, and I fear I've said too much.

"Can I ask you something?" she says, toying with a lock of dark hair, twisting it around her finger.

"Sure." I nod.

"It's about, um, sex stuff." Her cheeks flush the slightest bit, and I'm pretty sure it's because of whatever's running through that inquisitive brain of hers and not an effect of the hot water.

"Uh." My brain short-circuits momentarily as I struggle to find a reason this conversation shouldn't be happening right now. I come up blank.

*Fantastic.*

"I know you've had sex with at least four girls," she adds, her tone certain, a little bossy.

I almost chuckle, then catch myself. "Do you now?"

My number is easily north of twenty, but I'm not going to correct her. It's not necessarily a number I'm proud of—I went a little wild in college—and my stepsister really doesn't need this information because I know for a fact she'd start asking questions, and that's really not something I want.

"Yup. That girl Chloe you dated your freshman year, and then Tessa, sophomore year." She ticks them off on her fingers. "Then Bethany who you brought home for Thanksgiving—you said she was just a friend, but I heard noises coming from your bedroom that night."

Bethany was just a friend. She also gave great head.

I lean back in the water. "Okay so maybe I haven't been a saint, but I'm trying to be a good brother here."

Isla makes a noise of disagreement. "You are *not* my brother. Gross, Morgan. I'm just asking for some pointers, that's all."

I certainly don't feel very brotherly toward her. "Fine, what do you want to know?"

She takes a long drink of her beer before setting it on the edge of the hot tub. "I think part of the problem is that I… um, never made Tyler come."

*Nope. Hell no. This entire conversation is a hard pass.*

"Yeah, I'm not talking about this." I rise to my feet and swing one leg over the side of the hot tub to climb out. Isla reaches out to stop me, her warm palm connecting with my abs. There are six of them, each clearly defined; I work hard to keep it that way, and they tighten when her fingertips drag across them.

A bolt of electricity zings through me, snapping south.

She swallows, and pulls her hand away, as if realizing she's touching my bare skin. I've always been careful around her, and I can see now that inviting her to join me in the hot tub while drinking was not a good judgment call on my part. My bad.

It's time to go inside. Possibly take a cold shower. Or perform a lobotomy so I can erase this entire conversation from my brain.

Isla never made Tyler come.

She's asking me for tips on how to make a guy come.

Fuck. My. Life.

# CHAPTER TWO

*Morgan*

After my overly long and definitely colder than usual shower, I'm only slightly more clear-headed. I'm not proud to admit that I also rubbed one out in the shower, but it is what it is. And I'm trying desperately not to feel weird about that, or that Isla crossed my mind more times than she should have.

But come on. Technically, Isla's not family. She's just a hot as fuck nineteen-year-old with great tits who wants to drink my beer, prance around in a bikini and talk to me about sex. And as I said, I'm not a saint. I'm far fucking from it.

After dressing in black athletic shorts and a

white T-shirt, I make my rounds through the house, locking doors and turning off the lights. It's not even ten yet, but I'm guessing both Isla and I are ready to turn in for the night, considering she's not in the hot tub anymore and silence had fallen over the house. I wonder if she showered. I also wonder if she got herself off too.

*Not your business, man.*

Deciding that I need to man up and be the adult in this situation, I climb the stairs two at a time and head across the hall to Isla's bedroom instead of my own. I intend to check in on her, make sure she's okay, and say goodnight. That's it. Then I'm locking myself in my room and thinking about dying kittens or receiving a career ending injury. Anything to stop the insane and highly inappropriate images of Isla that seem to have taken root in my fucked-up head.

The door is closed, and I knock twice, and then step back and wait.

After a few moments, it opens and Isla stands before me dressed in a baggy sweatshirt that's falling off one shoulder and a tiny pair of pink boxer shorts that show off her long, toned legs. I force my eyes up and off of the miles of smooth skin on display.

"Hey," I say, voice coming out gruff. "I just wanted to check on you. Are you okay?"

She lifts her bare shoulder, eyes on mine. "I guess." Her eyes are such a pretty shade of blue. It's one of the first things I noticed about her when we first met many years ago. They're like the color of the sky after a storm. It's striking and I'll admit that I could happily stare into them for hours.

"I'm sorry if I was a dick before," I say, my eyes meeting hers. "Your question just took me off guard."

Her fingers curl around the edge of the door-frame she's leaning against. "It's okay. It was stupid of me to ask you. Of course you're not going to help me."

*Fuck.* Now I feel even more like an asshole. I could at least talk to her, answer her sex questions, even if it is a little tense between us and, yeah uncomfortable as fuck.

"Listen, I overreacted before. We can talk. I'll answer your questions. Sound okay?"

"Really?" Her full lips part and she smiles, and those gorgeous eyes of hers sparkle like twinkling stars. "Thank you, Morgan!" She leaps up on her toes to throw her arms around me. She practically tackles me with her excitement. Her excitement at the thought of talking about sex with me. *Yay*...I think bitterly.

I bring one muscled arm around her trim waist, feeling for the first time how well she fits against me, then quickly release her.

She leads the way into her room, and I sit down on the edge of her bed. I've never been in her bedroom before. It's not as girly as I expected. The walls are painted dark gray and her bedding is light gray and white. She's hung a painting of a colorful llama on the wall across from her bed.

"I love llamas," she says when she catches me looking at it.

"Who doesn't?" I grin at her, not hiding the amusement lingering on my words.

"You're making fun of me again," she says, lips pursed.

"Llamas are mean as shit. Everyone knows that."

"They're not mean," she defends. "Look how cute he is in the picture."

There is absolutely nothing cute about llamas. It actually looks mean. I shrug. "I've heard they spit on people."

She waves off my comment as if I've lost my mind before sitting on the bed across from me and crisscrosses her legs. I see a peek of her pale pink panties and quickly pull my gaze away. *Jesus, Morgan, focus.*

"So." She straightens her posture like she's a star pupil vying for the teacher's attention. "As I was saying before. I think one of the reasons Tyler broke up with me was because I never made him come."

Fucking hell, we are going straight into I see. I grit my teeth together. "Right."

She smiles. "I mean, I tried. Trust me, I did. With my hands and my mouth." But then she shakes her head, her smile falling away. "Not with my pussy though. I was saving it, as I mentioned, for Valentine's Day."

I've died and gone to heaven. Or maybe this is hell? Because Isla is talking about using her hands and her pussy to get off her dickless ex and I want nothing more than to push her back on the bed and show her how easy it would be to make me come, in spite of my release not even fifteen minutes ago.

*Goddamn it! Focus, Morgan.* This is not about

you or your dick.

I clear my throat, realizing she's waiting for me to say something—to impart some wisdom that will make sense of this crazy exchange between us.

"Right. Well, it's generally just a matter of pressure and speed." I'm thankful my voice sounds steady and composed, so I continue. "All guys are a little bit different, I'd imagine. But the idea is the same. You just need to communicate—find out what he likes and what feels good. Honestly, in my opinion, he should have just shown you. He sounds like kind of an asshole, leaving you to guess like that."

At this, she chuckles, her cheeks flushing the slightest bit. "Yeah… maybe."

"Maybe he had something wrong with him physically, Isla. Maybe it wasn't you at all."

She puts her fingertip on her lips. "Hm. I never thought of that."

I nod. "You never know." The guy sounds like a fucking douche, that's for certain. Isla is sweet, and kind, and beautiful. And she was willing to give him her virginity. I'm suddenly glad she didn't. Not that it's any of my business who she chooses to sleep with and give that precious gift to.

She's quiet for a minute, and I can't help the next words that fall out of my mouth. "Did he ever get you off?"

Those stormy blue eyes latch onto mine, and something inside me twists when she utters her next word.

"No."

It's not even really a word, more a breathless sound she makes. And I feel it all the way down in the pit of my stomach.

My throat feels tight, and I draw a slow, shallow breath while my heartbeat drums out a steady rhythm inside my chest. "Have you ever had an orgasm, Isla?"

She nods. "With myself, yes. Never with anyone else. I think I get too self-conscious or something."

*Damn.* The idea of her making herself come is the hottest thing ever and I know for certain that it's going to feature highly in my jack off reel for years to come. "It could have been the same for him. Maybe he was just nervous." I can't believe I'm making excuses for this dickhead.

"But you don't have that problem," Isla says,

voice soft.

She meets my eyes again, this time with a hungry look.

*Hungry for knowledge, Morgan, not your dick.*

*Get your head in the game.*

"Sex has always kind of come naturally for me," I admit with a shrug, desperate to bring back some casualness to the conversation because it feels like we're skating close to dangerous territory.

She chews on her lower lip, considering this. "How old were you when you lost your virginity?"

I consider blowing off her question, but she's been so open and honest tonight, I can't bring myself to lie to her.

"Fifteen," I admit.

"Wow!" She laughs, and her eyes sparkle yet again. "*Holy shit, Mor.*"

I chuckle. "Yeah. Freshman year of high school." I also lasted all of about three seconds, but I don't think I need to be quite *that* honest with her right now.

Things grow quiet between us, so quiet that I can hear the steady thrum of her heartbeat as she sits across from me, I can see her pulse racing against her neck.

She pushes out her tits as she shifts on the bed, and *fuck*, I want them in my hands. In my mouth. Against my chest.

My gaze drifts down to the front of her parted legs again and I catch another glimpse of her panties. I can't help but wonder if the conversation we're having has made her wet right now.

*What the hell is wrong with me?*

*Of course it's not. We're just talking.*

*So why is my dick all perked up in interest and already half hard?*

*Good fucking question.*

"Morgan?" She raises up onto her knees and crawls closer to me until she places one hand flat against my chest. I can feel the heat of her skin searing me through the thin material of my T-shirt. "Don't freak out, okay?"

"Why's that?" I ask, voice husky.

"Because I want to try something, okay?"

I don't answer. I don't move. I don't even fucking breathe as she lowers her plump mouth to mine and leans in for a chaste kiss.

I don't respond right away, mostly because I'm completely stunned. But then Isla parts her lips and teases the seam of mine with her tongue. It's instinct when my lips part and I touch my tongue to hers.

She lets out a low groan, and I deepen the kiss, threading my fingers through the silky hair at the back of her neck.

Then my brain snaps back on and I pull away, heart pounding and cock throbbing. "We can't."

She nods. "I know. I just wanted to see what it was like to kiss you."

"Why?" My brows crease.

Isla licks her lips, her tongue touching where mine just was, and I feel a sudden pang of jealousy. "Because I've always wondered what it'd be like to be with a guy who knew what he was doing. And I can tell you do."

She's not wrong. I know I could make her come. Probably in the next three minutes if I wanted to. But I won't. Some lines cannot be crossed, no matter how close we're skating to the edge.

"Can you just tell me a little bit more about

what you meant before about pressure… speed… I need to know how to make a guy come next time."

My eyes sink closed and I draw a frustrated breath. "Why don't you just watch a porn video or something?"

Isla shrugs. "I have. But I want some hands-on practice with an actual person so when the time comes I don't look like some inexperienced idiot."

My cock hardens fully, thickening against my thigh, and I pray she doesn't notice that the motherfucker is practically standing at attention, volunteering as tribute.

And then everything changes with the next words out of my mouth and it's clear that I've officially lost my fucking mind.

"One time Isla, and this never happens again. You got it?" My voice sounds way too low and gruff for my liking but fuck it.

Her eyes go wide as she realizes exactly what I'm offering.

"Yes, absolutely. Deal." She grins like she just won the fucking lottery.

# CHAPTER THREE

*Morgan*

**B**efore I can reconsider, I draw my shorts down my hips and my cock springs free. Isla sucks in a sharp inhale, her eyes glued to my crotch. I stand here like a statue, unable to move, unable to even breathe, except for the shaking, halted gasps leaving my lungs.

"Oh, it's…"

She doesn't finish that sentence, but what she does do makes my toes curl. Running her palm lightly against my steely shaft, she traces her thumb along the crown.

*Jesus.*

"How do I…" she starts.

"Wrap it in your fist." If I'd been uneasy at first, you wouldn't know it. My voice comes out rough and commanding, and like a good little student, Isla aims to please, curling her hand around me firmly. Even tentative, her touch sends heat rioting through my veins. One simple touch shouldn't feel this good. But holy shit…

I force a deep breath into my lungs, and then I wrap my hand around hers and demonstrate the motion, sliding slowly up, then down. "Like this," I say, voice a harsh pant.

She smiles at me shyly before those stormy eyes drop to my lap again. I try to see what she's seeing—eight inches of swollen flesh pulses crudely inside her small fist. It's obscene. And erotic. And hot as fuck.

"It's so much bigger than…" She grins, wickedly. "Never mind. I'll stop talking now."

I pinch the bridge of my nose and exhale as her movements grow faster.

It feels *so* good.

"That's it," I encourage, my voice little more

than a soft murmur. She meets my eyes with an appreciative expression.

Before I can process what's happening next, Isla lowers her head to my lap.

A helpless eager noise pushes past my lips just as her tongue licks along the vein in my shaft.

I watch in stunned fascination as she holds onto my cock and licks it like it's her favorite flavor lollipop. One long teasing lick along the crown, another slow lick down the side. A hot shiver rolls through me.

It's fucking torture.

The best kind of torture.

I grip the comforter in both fists, dropping back onto my elbows so I can watch her work me over.

She takes her time, tasting me shyly. It's nice, but I want more. "Swallow it."

Her eyes snap up to mine, filled with questions.

"The whole thing," I say.

She obeys, pushing her head down until I touch the back of her throat and she gags lightly around my length, withdrawing slowly.

I curse and take a shaky breath.

"Like that?" she asks, coming up for air.

There's a smear of spit on her lower lip and I wipe it away with my thumb. "Yeah. Exactly like that."

"And that would make you come?"

*So fucking hard.* "Yes."

"Even though I gagged?"

*Especially because you gagged.* What the fuck is wrong with me that I like choking her with my dick?

"Yes, Isla."

She goes back to work, lowering her mouth to my cock again, sucking me with such prideful determination it makes my abs tighten.

Unable to resist touching her tempting body any longer, I bring one hand under her sweatshirt and cup her warm tits in my hand. They're bare and bouncing slightly with the motion of her movements. I tease and pinch her nipples as she sucks on my cock, earning me a whimpered moan that I feel deep in my balls.

She lifts her eyes to mine and the pleasure I see

reflected back at me makes my heart stutter. "If you come, do I swallow it... or?"

For a second, I just stare at her. I want to say something flirty like *spitters are quitters*, but fuck, I can't do that. This is *Isla*. I'm already going to hell.

"I can't let you make me come."

"Can't *let me?* Why in the world not? Isn't that the entire point?" Her hand doesn't stop its torment, slowly dragging up and down over my swollen cock. It feels incredible. "I told you I didn't know how to please my boyfriend and he broke up with me over it."

Fuck. *She's right.* That was the entire point of this erotic experiment. She said she wanted practice. I stupidly agreed to be her guinea pig.

"Trust me, I'm close. You keep doing that, and I'm going to blow," I force out, a little breathless.

She looks pleased with herself, a slight smile forming on those beautiful full lips of hers.

I skim my fingers along the side of her breast.

"Fuck, Isla," I groan, watching the way her hand moves. Her fist doesn't even fully close around my thick shaft, and her thumb teases the pre-cum at the tip on each upstroke. Desperate horny noises escape the back of my throat and I fight off a shiver. I'm close. So close.

"Fuck, *fuck*," I heave, pushing her hand out of the way to finish myself with short, jolting strokes as thick spurts pulse out, coating my hand and lower abs.

"Oh," Isla inhales, bringing her fingertip to the warm mess on my stomach and painting a distracting-as-fuck figure-eight through it. "It's so messy," she murmurs, voice full of teasing pride.

"Be right back," I say, jumping up from the bed. I head into the adjoining bathroom and grab a wad of tissue which I use to clean myself up. Then I wash my hands and dry them on one of her towels.

When I join her on the bed again, Isla has removed her shirt and all my resolve about stopping this weakens.

"Jesus," I groan, running one hand through my hair.

Her tits are perfect, high and perky with pale peach-colored nipples. Isla makes room on the bed beside her and I sit down right next to her. "You're beautiful," I say, softly touching the bare skin of her shoulder. I still can't believe she's offering herself up this way, and my hands drift lower. Her breasts are so full in my palms, and as I massage them, she makes a surprised noise of pleasure. What I really want to do is nuzzle them with my face, and suck them into my mouth, but I'm still testing the waters and trying to make myself go slow.

Her knees part, her legs dropping open, and I have little doubt about what she wants next. But still, I need her to vocalize it, because this is pretty fucked up. Even for me.

"Are you sure you want this?" I ask, tracking one fingertip lightly over her bare thigh.

Little chill-bumps break out over her skin.

She nods, eager. "So much."

"Take off your shorts and panties," I say.

She wastes no time stripping down and then sits back down on the bed beside me. Isla is now naked while I'm once again fully clothed.

"Spread your legs."

She does and the sight makes my mouth water. She's pink and flushed with arousal—her gorgeous pussy is wet—and I want to bury my face in it.

But I don't.

I can't.

*Can I?*

*Shit.*

"How do you make yourself come?" I ask, fighting for control.

She bites her lip, and I wonder if she's going to answer. She's probably too shy. But then, rather than tell me, Isla shows me. Placing the pads of her fingers against her clit, she begins a slow erotic massage. "I touch myself right here," she says, voice choppy.

My brain almost short-circuits. *Jesus, that's hot.*

"That's good. It's important to know what you like, what feels good." My voice is barely above a whisper.

I watch, breathless, as her fingers move faster, rubbing herself.

Leaning forward, I capture one perky nipple in my mouth and give it a long tug. Isla whimpers, her hips bucking wildly.

I nuzzle and kiss and lightly bite both breasts as she works herself toward orgasm.

My hands move up and down over her firm thighs, but I don't touch between her legs. I just keep worshipping her breasts with my mouth until she's close, and then I move her hand out of the way. Her eyes snap open in confusion. I bring her fingertips to my mouth and suck them clean. She tastes so sweet, my cock starts to harden again.

Using my thumbs, I part her and touch her with soft strokes, with the same pressure I know she likes, thanks to her erotic demonstration.

Isla's hips rock, and throaty cries fall from her lips. I won't let myself penetrate her. I have no right to know how tight and perfect she'd feel around my fingers, but I am going to be the one to make her come.

A few more seconds, and she starts to unravel, her body twitching and tightening as she moans out my name. Her orgasm crashes through her, and it's the most beautiful thing I've ever seen.

# CHAPTER FOUR

*Morgan*

"**A**re you sure you're okay?" I ask once she's dressed again. After our little experiment where I learned that not only can Isla definitely one-hundred percent make a man come but she also looks fucking incredible when she comes undone, she'd gone to the bathroom, brushed her teeth and then climbed into bed.

She nods from her pillow where I've tucked her in with the fluffy blanket pulled up to her chin. "I'm sleepy." She lets out a huge yawn and I chuckle.

Post-orgasmic bliss looks good on her.

This whole situation should probably feel strange. It should feel all kinds of wrong and taboo, but the thing is, it just doesn't. I keep waiting for it to hit me, just like I keep waiting for her to freak out. But she looks content, complete and utterly content and satisfied.

I take a step back and turn off the lamp. The dim hallway light provides just enough lighting to illuminate the room. Standing at the side of her bed, I look down at her and hesitate.

"Are you sure you feel okay about everything that happened?"

Isla smile is soft as she stares up at me, nodding. "I'm happy and totally okay. Thanks for tonight, Morgan, it meant a lot to me."

Something tightens in my chest as I watch her curl into the pillow, releasing a sleepy exhale as she snuggles deeper into her bed.

"Let's talk in the morning, okay?"

She nods. "Can we go out for pancakes?"

I chuckle, completely fucking relieved that she's not upset or regretting that things went too far between us tonight. "Of course we can."

"And bacon?" she asks, sleepily.

"Abso-fucking-lutely." I chuckle.

Isla grins. "Goodnight Morgan," she says, turning on her side.

"Goodnight sweet Isla," I murmur before turning to head for the door.

# CHAPTER FIVE

*Morgan*

It isn't until the next morning that the full weight of last night's activities hits me like a ton of bricks. A sexy, fucked up, totally unexpected ton of bricks. I wait for regret to rob me of the pleasant memories, but there's only a hazy sense of accomplishment at the idea that maybe I did actually help her.

I can hear Isla's shower running as I get up to brush my teeth, so I know she's up. The thought of her naked body conjures all the images from last night freshly to my mind, causing a stir of arousal in my boxer briefs. I wonder how she's feeling about it all now that she's had a good night sleep to process it. If she hasn't come bursting through my door demanding an apology for violating her last night, that has to be a good sign, right?

After a quick rinse in the shower, I throw on a pair of jeans and a T-shirt and head down to the kitchen. I promised her pancakes and a debriefing in the morning, and if last night taught us anything, I'm a man who's true to my word. And then some.

Just as I'm finishing my cup of coffee, I hear Isla padding across the hall and down the stairs. I brace myself for a confrontation, for her to be embarrassed or shy or angry. But when she appears around the corner wearing jeans and a scoop neck sweater that make me want to do all kinds of bad things to her, she gives me the same regular smile she always does. Like she didn't have her hands and mouth on my cock just twelve hours ago. Like I hadn't touched her in places that made her moan my name and shudder as she came hard. But when my eyes meet hers, oddly enough everything feels… normal. A little bit sexually charged, but normal. Like what we did last night was as casual as going out to get pancakes and bacon this morning.

Okay, that was unexpected.

"Morning, Morgan," she says, happily, pouring herself a cup of coffee.

"Good morning, Isla." Instead of focusing on her stunning face, I zoom in on the extra large cup she's pouring coffee into. "I didn't realize you were a coffee drinker."

She shoots me an incredulous look. "I'm a college student, not a freak of nature."

I shrug and raise my hands in surrender. "How fast can you finish that cup? I'm starving."

She rolls her eyes, but downs her coffee in record time, and then the two of us climb into my truck, chatting easily the whole way to the diner. Once there, we're seated in a booth by the windows and place our orders.

"I'll have the pancake breakfast with bacon and an orange juice," Isla says with a smile, handing her menu to the waitress.

"I'll do the lumberjack's special, eggs over easy and hash browns well done. And can I get pancakes instead of toast?" I ask, winking at Isla.

"Sure thing, sweetie," the waitress replies, tucking my menu under her arm.

As she walks away, Isla leans toward me, resting her elbows on the table in a way that puts her full breasts on perfect display.

"Damn, Morgan, think you'll have enough food?" she teases.

"Hey, a man's got to eat," I say with a shrug, forcing my eyes away from her chest.

She smiles and shakes her head. "Are all hockey players such bottomless pits?"

I think of the massive team dinners we go to together, where our table is always jammed packed with food, which always has a way of disappearing quickly.

"Yeah, you could say we tend to have big appetites."

Isla chuckles. "Of I've heard the stories about hockey players…you don't just have big appetites for food. I know about the puck bunnies, Mor," she chuckles, fiddling with her napkin. "Have you had an girlfriends since you've moved to Seattle? Do you want one?" she asks, looking up at me with a curious expression.

"Uh…" I hesitate, my voice strained. "Not sure."

The waitress returns with my coffee and her orange juice, and we settle into comfortable conversation, finally learning all the things about each other we never got around to. We've never spent much time together, and the times we did, I spent so much of it trying to avoid her, avoid noticing how sexy she was, it's nice just to have a regular conversation. I have to say, it's pretty cool being able to finally open up and learn more about her.

"I had no idea you were thinking about a political science minor," I say before shoveling another bite of pancake into my mouth.

"It was Tyler's idea, actually. But that doesn't matter anymore, I guess."

The mention of Tyler snaps my attention back to last night. I watch her face closely for any trace of shame or regret, but I don't find either. I decide to move past it and let her be the one to bring it up.

"I'm sorry about the breakup. Even if the guy turned out to be a worthless piece of shit, it still sucks to go through."

She shrugs, poking around at her pancakes with her fork. "It weirdly doesn't even bother me anymore. I think last night might have something to do with it."

I give her a long, measured look and can't help the way my mouth tilts in a slight grin. "In a good way?"

She locks eyes with me. "I think so."

*Not exactly the response I was looking for.*

"Look, Isla, I'm sorry if I pressured you into doing something you didn't want to do. It's just that—"

But before I can finish, she cuts me off, resting her hand on top of mine on the table.

"Don't apologize. I asked for your help. And that's exactly what you gave me. You helped." She grins at me. "Really helped."

I stare deep into her eyes, searching for any hint of a lie. "Are you sure? Because the last thing I want is for you to tell me what you think I want to hear right now." *Not to mention you did as much of the helping as I did.*

"I'm positive. I think it was exactly what I needed. Thank you, Morgan."

She gives me a soft smile, and I smile back.

"I should be thanking *you*. It's not like there wasn't anything in it for me, you know."

A pretty blush creeps over her chest and cheeks. "Trust me, I remember."

Just as I'm about to respond, my phone rings

in my pocket. When I pull it out to check it, I can't tell whether I want to burst out laughing or hide my face in shame.

Instead of doing either, I answer it. "Hi, Dad."

Isla practically snorts orange juice through her nose. I silently shush her while my dad goes through all the normal greetings, and she claps a hand over her mouth, her eyes wide with equal parts amusement and horror.

"So, how's Isla doing?" he asks. "Have the two of you seen much of each other this weekend?"

*Oh, we've seen plenty.*

"Isla's good. She's right here, actually, if you want to talk to her."

Her eyes grow somehow even wider, and she shakes her head in disbelief.

My dad sounds pleasantly surprised. "She is? Well, look at you two, finally getting to spend a little quality time together. Did you hear that, Dawn? The kids are spending time together."

I cringe at the sound of my dad calling us "the kids," but quickly shrug it off as Isla's mother takes the phone.

"Oh, Morgan, I'm so happy to hear that! Thank you for taking such good care of my baby girl."

*You have no idea.*

"It's my pleasure, Dawn."

I can hear the smile in her voice when she replies. "So, you guys got to know each other better?"

*Biblically speaking? Yes.*

"Uh-huh," I stammer. "Would you like to talk to her?"

I hand the phone to Isla, who rolls her eyes at me before forcing a smile on her face to talk to her mother.

"Hi, Mom. Yes, Morgan and I are out getting breakfast right now. I know, it *is* about time we got to know each other, isn't it?" She nods along as they talk, her tone casual and even, but the longer they talk, the look on her face grows more and more embarrassed while her eyes grow increasingly heated.

"Uh-huh, you're right, we should have given each other a chance a long time ago. But hey, some things can't be rushed, you know?" She winks at me, sending a jolt of electricity behind my zipper.

This girl never ceases to surprise me.

She continues to nod as they wrap up their conversation. "Okay, sounds good. Have fun, you guys! Bye."

She hangs up and hands the phone back to me.

"They say goodbye and thank you," she says, the corner of her mouth lifting into a smile.

"They're, uh, welcome?"

We lock eyes, pausing for a moment before bursting out laughing, the tension of the last five minutes too much to handle any longer.

Isla looks at me and shakes her head, her smile slowly fading into a satisfied look. "That was insane."

I shrug. "What they don't know won't kill them."

"God, I hope so."

We finish our meal and I pay at the counter, both of us still smiling in disbelief the whole ride home. Once there, we linger in the kitchen before parting ways.

"I should probably get going soon. Long drive ahead of me," I say, nodding to my room upstairs.

"Yeah, you don't want to hit any traffic," she replies, crossing her arms and leaning against the counter.

I start to walk away, but something stops me. I turn back around, running a hand over the back of my neck. "Hey, listen, I just want to let you know that you shouldn't let any of that Tyler bullshit weigh you down once you get back to school. You're an amazing catch, Isla and he's an idiot for letting you go."

She smiles as her cheeks flame red. "Thanks, Morgan. That's nice of you to say."

"I mean it. Shit, if you want a professional hockey team to beat him up, I'm just a phone call or text away."

She laughs. "I don't think that'll be necessary. I'm pretty good with my fists."

*Damn if I don't know that by now.*

"Well, if there's anything you need, feel free to call or text me anytime. And I mean, *whatever* you might need—just to talk or whatever." *Yep, I'm definitely going to hell.*

A coy smile forms on her lips. "Careful, Morgan. I just might take you up on that."

"Trust me, Isla. I hope you will."

# CHAPTER SIX

*Morgan*

**M**y phone buzzes and the name flashing on the screen sends a jolt of nervous energy down my spine.

*Isla.*

I take a deep breath and tap the screen to view the message, half-hoping she's texting me to let me know she can't make it. It would certainly make things a lot easier. A lot more clear cut. Because anytime her name appears on my phone screen, I get this strange heart-fluttering feeling. Weird, right?

```
Hey! Just letting you know we're
leaving now. Can't wait to see
```

you soon! :)

I guess that answers my question.

My dad, along with Isla and her mom, are on their way to Seattle to stay with me this weekend. It's been a year since *that* night at our parents' house, and while we've seen each other a couple of times since then, our parents were always around to ease the tension that swam between us. Not that they have any idea what happened. Hell no. If anything, they're just excited that the four of us can all hang out now like adults. I don't even want to think about what would happen if they found out what I taught her that weekend they were out of town on their honeymoon.

But let's be honest, I wouldn't mind giving her another lesson. I've thought about it so many times, I'm surprised I haven't rubbed all the skin off my dick in the process.

That's not what this weekend is about, though. Because while we might not have seen each other very often, we've stayed in touch, texting a couple times a week about her classes, my hockey schedule, and everything in between. Much to my surprise, she even started letting me know when she used some of the techniques I showed her in the bedroom. Nothing too graphic, but I got the picture… and got more turned on than I'd like to admit.

So when she texted me complaining about having no plans for spring break, I didn't think twice about inviting her to Seattle. My team has a huge game this weekend, and no matter how we do, we always like to go out and have some fun afterward, whether we're celebrating a victory or drowning our sorrows. It might not be on the same level as enjoying an umbrella drink in Cancun, but I'll make sure she has a damn good time.

My phone buzzes again and this time it's Owen, reminding me about our pre-game meeting this afternoon. Our coach has been on a sports psychology kick this season, and he decided that this weekend was a good time to try out some pre-competition meditation techniques. It sounds like a bunch of hippy-dippy bullshit to me, but I don't make the rules. The only problem is I totally forgot about the meeting, and it's at the same time that Isla's supposed to get here.

```
Gonna be late. Parentals and
    stepsister coming to visit.
```

Before hitting send, I pause at the word "stepsister" glaring at me from my phone. That's technically what Isla is to me, but it feels like the wrong way to describe our relationship. After going back and forth about it, I delete the word and replace it with "friend." Less complicated. And makes me feel about ten thousand times less creepy.

I spend the next two hours cleaning my apartment and making it presentable for my house guests. My dad and stepmom will sleep in the newly furnished guest room. I'm thankful for some of my female friends, mainly Aubree and Bailey, for forcing me into furnishing it—it's got a queen-sized bed and dresser now at least.

Isla will sleep on the couch. Aside from the not-so-subtle hints she drops from time to time thanking me for the lesson I gave her, we haven't ever talked about being physical again. Don't get me wrong, my attraction to her hasn't faded one single bit, but the last thing I want is for her to feel obligated to do anything. This weekend is about hanging out with the family, not getting my dick sucked.

My phone dings. It's Isla.

We're here!

Here goes nothing.

I buzz them in, listening to their footsteps coming up the stairwell while my heart pounds out an erratic rhythm in my chest.

*Geez, chill the fuck out, Mor.*

Dad gives me a hug and when he releases me, I take the duffle bag from Isla's hands and have to force my eyes away, because *damn* does she look incredible. Toned legs encased in a pair of well-fitting jeans. A tight ass that I would love to become better acquainted with, a shy smile, and eyes that communicate so much. Ignoring the simmering attraction between us, I give everyone a tour of my place.

"You've grown muscles on top of your muscles," my stepmom Dawn says, pulling me in for a hug. "How have you been, honey?"

Regular team workouts and fighting to keep a spot in the pros will keep you in good shape, that's for certain. "I've been great."

I can't help my gaze from straying to Isla as I make small talk with my dad and Dawn. I wonder what she's thinking about as her eyes roam around my apartment.

As Dad carries their suitcases into the guest room, he calls over his shoulder, "It's a good thing you have a second bedroom, Isla's applied for an internship in the city this summer. You guys could end up being roommates."

My head snaps over to look at Isla. A shy smile tugs at her lips.

"That's amazing," I say, trying to act casual. Isla as a roommate? Why does that thought make my heart pound? "Also, hi. I'm glad you're here." I realize as the words leave my mouth, they're one-hundred percent true. I had been nervous about this, but somehow, seeing her here, it just feels right.

"Hi to you too," she chuckles, breaking some of the tension between us.

Shoving my hands through my hair, I glance at the clock in the kitchen. "I'm sorry, I've got to run. Pre-game meeting. But I'll see at the arena. And there's food in the fridge, so help yourself to anything."

"Kick some ass tonight," Dad says, flashing me a proud grin.

I grab my stuff and head out, pausing to make sure my dad has the tickets for tonight I sent.

I make it through the pre-game meditation and the warmup. And now it's finally game time. All the lights in the stadium have been dimmed for the national anthem, and I have to squint out at the crowd to try and find the seats my friend Becca got for my dad, Dawn, and Isla. My dad is easy to spot. He's the tallest of the three and dressed in a forest green jersey with my number on it. My throat gets a little tight as I watch him with his hand over his heart. I'm really freaking glad he came. Next to him is my stepmom, who's got a huge smile, and then beside her is Isla. Her eyes are locked onto mine and a small shiver races through me. I'm glad she's here too.

Once the game starts and our first line takes the ice, the action passes by in a blur. I get little in the way of playing time, but I'm thankful even for that. Our roster is stacked with the country's top talent, and I'm one of the newer, younger guys on the team. Just because I'm hungry for more ice time doesn't mean it'll be handed to me. I'll have to earn it, and I intend to. I wasn't raised to be an entitled asshole, I was raised to work hard and appreciate what you've got. And what I've got is a pretty sweet gig considering I get to play a game I love for a living. I watch the action out on the ice, trying to spot the openings, the opposing team's weaknesses.

After the game ends—a three to one win for

us—we go out to dinner with our parents. Isla fills us in on college and the possibility of this internship, and the small talk flows easily throughout the night.

A few hours later, our parents have gone home and now I'm sitting across from Isla in one of the red vinyl booths in the back of Dicky's dive bar, one of our team's favorite post-game spots in Seattle. The one thing I didn't think about when I invited her to come out with us was the fact that she'd be meeting my teammates. My horny, booze-loving, dick-swinging teammates. Which means I've spent the last hour playing goalie off the ice too, trying to keep their wandering sticks from getting tangled in Isla's net. Most of them are in relationships now, but I'm not sure how that would stop them from noticing how gorgeous she is. And I definitely don't like the way the rookie left-winger Jordie is looking at her. If it wouldn't make such a scene, I'd fucking punch him.

"Morgasm, how come you never told us you have a sister?" Teddy drawls, slapping me on the back. I roll my eyes at the new nickname, shrugging his hand off of me.

"Because he doesn't," Isla interjects, propping her elbows on the table and leaning forward.

Teddy squints between the two of us.

"But…"

"Our parents got married when I was seventeen. Morgan was away at college. We never lived together and didn't really even start getting to know each other until more recently." She shrugs, downing the rest of her drink. "We're more like friends than anything."

I don't think I've ever heard her talk about me to someone else before. Honestly? It's pretty hot.

"Gotcha," Teddy mumbles, taking another swig of his beer.

Isla smiles politely at him before looking past him, her eyes wandering over the crowded bar. I check my phone for the time since I promised our parents I wouldn't keep her out too late. Suddenly, those eyes are looking at me, and the look they're giving sends an electric shock right through me, straight to my groin.

*Holy shit.*

"So, *Morgasm*," she says, her nose crinkling at the nickname, "what do you say you and I do a shot? In the name of winning the game and all."

My teammates hoot and holler at the challenge,

and the two of us slide out of the booth to make our way to the bar, our bodies pressed closely together in the crowded space. I watch with wonder as Isla sidles up to the bartender, leaning her narrow frame over the counter to point out exactly what she wants. Soon she's turning back to me, two shot glasses in hand with some kind of mysterious clear liquid inside.

"What is this? Vodka?" But she doesn't answer, instead clinking her glass to mine and tossing it back. I follow suit, the taste that hits my tongue a shock to me—because there isn't one.

"Was that fucking water?"

She giggles and nods, arching toward me to talk in my ear.

"I had to make sure we stay hydrated somehow."

We laugh, and all I can do is shake my head. You can take a nerd out of the library…

Isla swivels back toward me with two new shot glasses, this time filled with a liquid so pink it almost looks like it's glowing.

"Please tell me that's not just water with food coloring in it."

She shakes her head, giving me the same look she gave me at the booth, the one that keeps feeding the gnawing ache in my gut I've felt from the moment she got here.

"It's a wet pussy."

It's all I can do to not let my mouth fall open at the sound of that word coming out of her mouth. It's maybe the sexiest thing I've ever heard—and judging by the sudden tightness in my jeans, my dick thinks so too.

"Cheers," she says, lifting her chin in a nod before tossing the shot back, licking the few stray drops from her lower lip.

I watch her for a moment before doing the same, hardly able to tear my eyes away from her face.

"Do you want to get out of here?"

The words leave my lips before I can think about them. My head is spinning, but something tells me it has more to do with Isla and less to do with whatever was in that shot.

She nods, so I take her hand in mine and lead her through the crowd, ducking past my teammates and through the door. We call a car and climb into the backseat, the music from the radio thumping too loudly for us to talk. Not that we need to. We're sitting close together, her thigh pressing into mine. It takes every ounce of self-control in me not to crush my mouth against her right there in the back of the Uber. But Isla hasn't touched me all night, and even if she has been a little flirty, that certainly doesn't mean something is going to happen between us. Maybe that was a one-time thing. I could live with that.

When we get home, my apartment is dark and quiet.

"The parental units must be in bed," I whisper.

Isla nods and slips off her shoes by the door.

The open floor plan provides a clear view into the living room, which will be her room for the night. Apparently Dawn has made up the couch for her, because there are blankets and pillows all set up neatly.

"You need anything?"

Isla shakes her head. "'Night, Morgan." Lifting up on her toes, she presses a sweet, slow kiss to my cheek. At the touch of her lips to my skin, I feel a slight tingle, but I pull back and meet her gaze.

"Goodnight."

Swallowing down a wave of desire, I walk to my bedroom and close the door. *Alone*. With a deep breath, I scrub my hands through my hair. I'm horny and a whole lot sexually frustrated, but there's absolutely nothing I can do about that.

After I wash my hands and brush my teeth in the adjoining bathroom, I enter my room again and turn off the light. I've just stripped out of my shirt when the door opens—a sliver of light from the hall faintly illuminating Isla's shy expression.

She closes my bedroom door behind her and crosses the room to stand before me.

"Hey, did you need something?" I ask, turning to toss my button-down shirt onto the chair beside my bed.

But when I turn around, the look in her eyes stops me. Hungry, searching. And really, really fucking sexy.

"I never thanked you," she says. "For teaching me."

"I, uh… what? Yes, you did."

She shakes her head, slowly closing the distance between us.

"I never thanked you… properly."

"You don't have to thank me for anything…. Trust me, it was my pleasure."

She runs her fingertips over the muscles in my chest, just barely grazing the skin. My cock twitches, and she's close enough to notice.

"You sure?" Her lips lift into a smile as she brings them centimeters from mine, so close I can feel her breath on my skin, smell the sweetness of her floral shampoo. She couldn't be further from the shy, sexually timid nineteen-year-old I encountered last year. Standing in front of me is a woman, fearless and strong, and this time, she knows what she wants.

The question is… am I willing to go there with our parents right across the hall?

# CHAPTER SEVEN

*Morgan*

Our mouths meet for the first time in a year, but it's so natural, it feels like it could have been yesterday. Isla is an amazing kisser—not too rushed, but not too slow either and her hot tongue strokes mine like she's eager for more. Everything below my waist hardens immediately.

Her fingers drift to the button on my pants and she slowly draws down my zipper. My cock bobs with pleasure even though she hasn't so much as touched it yet.

I should stop her. I have to stop her. There's no other choice.

A soft knock on my door causes us to pull apart.

Then a voice startles us apart.

"Son, a word, please?" It's my dad.

My eyes widen almost comically large and Isla staggers back like she's been slapped. She presses one hand over her mouth and shakes her head.

*Shit*. This isn't good. Our parents probably heard us in the next room. Talk about inappropriate family bonding. *What the hell was I thinking?*

"Uh," I say, buttoning up my pants and squeezing the base of my cock in an effort to get it to soften. It doesn't work of course. "Now's not a great time, Dad."

He chuckles, a dark mocking sound from behind the door. "Oh, I'm aware. But this will only take a second."

*Shit*. I draw a deep breath into my lungs and look at Isla. She looks panicked, like a deer caught in headlights times a million. Her eyes beg me not to let him in, but I shrug, what else can I do? Then I cross the room to the door and draw a deep breath. While uncertainty turns inside my stomach, I pull it open just a few inches and meet my dad's eyes reluctantly. But he doesn't look mad. Doesn't look upset at all. In fact, he's smiling.

"Hey," I say, voice a rough croak.

I'm about to launch into a full-court apology, about to admit what an obvious scum bag I am and beg for his forgiveness. But Dad's smile widens.

"Breathe, Morgan," he says.

I do, inhaling deeply as I steady myself with one hand braced against the door frame.

"Dawn went to the living room to say good-night to Isla, only she wasn't there."

I lick my lips. Of course she wasn't there. Because she was in my room, trying to wrestle my erection out of my boxer briefs.

I'm speechless, stunned into silence, but Dad continues. "Well, we kind of put two and two together. About why Isla was so excited to come on this weekend's trip. About the sweet smiles that grace her lips when she texts with you at the dinner table..."

"I, uh..." I stall, rubbing the back of my neck with one hand. *Fucking say something, dude!*

Dad holds up one hand, stopping me. "Let me finish."

I nod.

"All I wanted to say was that you're both adults. You're certainly not related... and as long as you treat her right, Isla's mother and I are in full support of this."

*Wait.* What? I must have heard him wrong. I blink twice, waiting for him to say something else. Only he doesn't.... Holy shit. He's serious. Our parents know? And they're cool with it? My knees almost buckle. That was so not what I was expecting him to say. I make another inarticulate sound.

Dad chuckles. "But, our room is right across the hall, and so even if we are in support of whatever this is between you two, your parents don't want to hear you going at it. Is that clear, son?"

"Crystal," I choke out, desperate to start breathing like a normal person again.

Dad nods once, smiling again, then calls around the door, "Goodnight, Isla."

"'Night, Frank," I hear from behind me.

When I close the door and turn to face her, Isla is laughing into her fist. "Oh my God!" she whisper-shrieks.

"Did that just happen?" I'm honestly not quite sure if I dreamed the entire thing.

She nods, eyes wide and locked on mine.

"That was so fucking weird."

"The weirdest," she confirms.

I fall back onto the bed, staring straight up at the ceiling, still reeling. Isla joins me, curling herself in next to me.

"Are you okay?" she chuckles, more amused than horrified by this whole thing.

"I don't know," I admit. "I think I'd be less surprised right now if my dad just admitted he was actually an alien sent from outer space."

Isla laughs again, then runs her hand down my chest, stopping at my waistband.

I catch her hand in mine. "It was also a total boner killer."

Not discouraged, she pulls her hand from my grasp, she places it right over my zipper, and strokes the soft bulge. "I might be able to do something about that."

Turning her chin toward mine so I can meet her eyes, I give my head a firm shake. "Are you insane? They can hear us. They're right across the hall."

Her lips press together teasingly. "Then I guess we'll have to be super quiet."

I give her an uncertain look.

"I'm up for the challenge. Are you?" she asks, drawing down my zipper before I can respond.

My breath gets stuck in my throat as Isla reaches one hand inside my boxer briefs and draws out my aching dick. I should push her away, stop her, do something... But I can't make the words leave my throat.

"Jesus, Morgan," she whispers. "Did this thing get bigger?"

Taking over, I stroke it once while her eyes widen. "Take off your shirt. The bra too," I say, lifting up on one elbow.

Isla is a good little student. Scratch that, she's the star pupil, because faster than I would have thought possible, she's stripped herself free of her shirt, lacy bra, and the skinny jeans she was wearing.

"Beautiful," I whisper.

Isla takes over, putting her hand over mine to stroke my cock again.

I suppress a chuckle as appreciation rolls through me. "We have to be quiet," I whisper.

She nods. "We will." Her voice is barely audible, giving me hope that maybe we can do this.

I bite my lip, watching her delicate hand move over me. "Put your mouth on it?"

She smiles and lowers her lips to my cock. "Happy to."

At the first wet stroke of her tongue, a groan rumbles in my chest. I touch her hair, brushing my fingers through the silky dark waves as I watch her work me over with admiration.

I fight off a hot shiver as she cradles my balls in one hand and strokes all the way down my cock with the other.

*Jesus, she's learned a thing or two since the last time we were together.*

"Gonna make me come," I groan out on a whisper.

Isla pulls off me with a wet sound. "I want to feel you inside of me," she whispers.

My body is screaming *yes, yes, yes.* My head, however, takes over, and I look down to meet her eyes. "Have you done that before?"

She nods. "Yes. There were two guys last year. I... *experimented*, after we, ya know...."

I nod. I don't need all the details. I just wanted to make sure she knew what she was really asking for.

"Are you sure that's what you want?"

She nods, slipping her panties down over her hips. "Get a condom."

*Damn.* That's hot.

I obey. Once it's on, I move over top of her, my length nudging her entrance as my lips touch the space between her neck and shoulder. My hips buck gently into her, and she whimpers in response. Encouraged, I press a kiss to her mouth. "You sure? We could do other stuff..."

She shakes her head. "I want you. I always have."

With a slow inhale to fill my lungs, I thrust up into the tightest heat I've ever felt and let out a low groan. Catching myself, I bite my lip and fight to stay quiet.

Isl. isn't as disciplined. At the first soft moan

she makes, I place my palm over her mouth covering it securely.

"Stay nice and quiet for me while I fuck you, okay?" I meet her eyes—they're dark and filled with her desire.

She nods, but I keep my hand pressed over her mouth. There's something insanely erotic about covering her mouth with my hand while I pump in and out of her in slow, steady thrusts.

She whimpers against my palm, meeting my eyes with a half-lidded gaze. She tilts her pelvis to meet mine and I sink all the way in, until there's no more separation between us, until there's just heat and electricity and. So. Much. Pleasure.

Part of me still can't believe this beautiful girl, who I'm insanely attracted to, is giving herself to me like this. I must be the luckiest bastard in the world.

"You feel so good," I whisper on a groan. "You're incredible. So sexy."

She nods once, her head bobbing with my palm still pressed against her lips. I know what she's saying. *You are too.*

I give my hips an experimental thrust, going

deep. Isla's breath catches in her throat.

"Can you stay quiet if I move my hand?"

She nods.

I remove my hand and then carefully change up our positions so I'm flat on my back and she's perched on top of me.

"You okay like this?" I whisper.

She nods again.

"I want to watch you ride me," I say with a cocky smirk, tucking my hands behind my head.

Rising to the challenge, Isla plants her palms against my abs and moves—bouncing against me with the most delicious friction moving up and down my shaft in a nice, steady rhythm.

Maybe I hadn't thought this position through, because watching her move above me, the way her breasts bounce, the soft skin of her belly leading down to the gorgeous sight between her legs, the way her chest rises with her quick inhalations... it does something to me.

*Shit.*

She's going to make me come too soon and disgrace myself.

"Fuck, Morgan," she moans, leaning over me so her breasts rub against my chest. The skin to skin contact feels incredible and all my nerve endings are raw. I'm not going to last. That much is certain.

She grabs a fistful of sheets in her hands, nuzzling her face into my neck. Her entire body is trembling.

"Come for me, Isla."

It's barely a few seconds later... and she obeys, tightening around me as her body quakes. She comes apart, unraveling completely, gasping in my arms while I hold her, and my orgasm quickly follows. I spill myself in hot, wet bursts into the end of the condom. I feel dizzy and breathless.

"That was incredible," I whisper, voice hoarse as I press a kiss to her temple.

A few moments later, after I've dealt with the condom, we're cuddled together in a breathless heap, her hair sticking to both of our skin. She curls into my side, her arm flung across my chest. I'm comfortable with her here in my space, and I like knowing that she feels comfortable with me too.

"Best night ever," she breathes, a smile floating on her lips. "Thank you, Morgan."

I turn to face her, brushing a few stray hairs from her forehead as I shake my head, still blown away by this amazing woman. "Thank *you.*"

She swallows, looking unsure for a moment. "So what happens now?" she asks.

I chuckle. That is a very good question. I never anticipated having a real shot with her. Never anticipated that our parents would be cool with us as a couple. But knowing that they are? It opens up a whole new realm of possibility.

"First off, you're staying the night in my bed, not on the couch."

She giggles. "Okay. And then after?"

"How about we discuss that over pancakes tomorrow morning," I suggest, tucking her in closer against me. "And bacon."

I can feel Isla's answering smile against my skin. "I think I'd like that."

# CHAPTER EIGHT

*Morgan*

I would like to tell you that the morning after wasn't awkward.

I would like to tell you that we all behaved like adults and everyone lived happily ever after...

The truth is far more twisted, however.

Isla and I awoke that morning to the sounds of grunting from across the hall. It had taken me a minute to place the sounds, mostly because I was half-asleep and no one's ever used my guest room quite so vigorously before. Isla, being smarter than me, realized instantly and her entire body had gone stiff in my arms.

Then I heard the bedsprings creaking, and ...

*Oh my God.*

Realization dawned.

Our parents were fucking in the room across the hall.

I could have lived my entire life and died happy not knowing that my dad liked to start the day with some energetic morning sex.

Isla sat up, shaking her head. Her hair was thoroughly tangled and she worked her fingers through it absently, not looking nearly as distraught as I felt.

"Is this payback for last night? Are they trying to give us a taste of our own medicine?" she asked, climbing from the bed to locate her clothes.

I heaved out an exhale and pressed my hands to my ears. "I have no fucking idea, but you wanna get out of here?"

Her eyes narrowed on mine. "And go where, exactly?"

She was right...I was suggesting we sneak out of my own apartment and hide out somewhere. Maybe forever.

"Out to breakfast," I suggested, remembering

that I'd promised her we'd talk about *us* over pancakes this morning.

"Okay," she agreed.

We got dressed and headed out. I nearly bumped into Dawn in the hall on her way to the bathroom. Holy awkward walk of shame. Her cheeks were stained hot and she looked down, mumbling something to herself that I couldn't quite catch. I didn't ask her to repeat herself. I just needed out of here as-soon-as-freaking-possible.

Isla stood wide-eyed by the front door waiting for me. Grabbing my shoes, I shuffled out after her as quickly as I could.

She gave my shoulder a playful shove once we were outside and smirked. "Like father like son..."

We burst into easy laughter after that, and the knot of tension in my stomach disappeared. That happened a lot when she was near. She had a way of making all the stress in my life vanish.

The way to the diner was spent laughing. And over pancakes and coffee I asked Isla to be my girlfriend. She beamed at me, blue eyes sparkling. "What are we going to tell people about how we met? We need a better story."

I nodded. That was true. I was guessing that "she's my stepsister ... and came begging for my cock one night" wasn't going to work too well. "I'll think of something," I promised, lifting her hand to my mouth and pressing a kiss to the back.

Her eyes met mine and communicated so much. She trusted me. She believed in me. And there was no better feeling in the world.

• • •

Want More?

If you enjoyed this short story and want more in the world of my sexy, brooding hockey players, be sure to check out the HOT JOCKS SERIES, beginning with book one, PLAYING FOR KEEPS. Each story is a standalone about a different member of the team.

Read on for a sneak preview

HOT JOCKS 1

# PLAYING FOR KEEPS

# CHAPTER ONE

Unruly Hockey Players

*Justin*

I have a beautiful woman sitting in my lap.

I don't know her name, or what she does for a living, or where she grew up.

I do know that she smells like tequila… and that tequila and I have never played particularly well together.

But none of that matters to her.

The only thing that matters is that I'm a pro hockey athlete, and so she's ready to fuck me. Which holds exactly zero appeal for me.

Don't get me wrong, I love female attention, but lately every minute of it all feels stale, like I've been there, seen that, done it all before and have the t-shirt to prove it.

I'm not even sure she knows my name. But I'd bet good money on her knowing my jersey number by heart. I guess that's why they call the women jersey chasers, or in hockey—puck bunnies.

"Justin Motherfuckin' Brady!" Owen, my best friend and roommate, calls from our living room. "Get a drink and get your balls in here."

I nod and flash him a thumbs-up.

"You'll have to excuse me," I say to the petite brunette currently running her hands down my chest.

She blinks at me with lust-filled blue eyes. After a moment's hesitation, she hops up from my lap with a frown and I slide off of the barstool.

"If you want to score tonight, I'm a sure thing, cutie," she says with a flirty wink.

I rub one hand over my jaw. This shit is really getting old. "I'm good. Thanks, though."

I'm sure I sound like an asshole, but whatever. I can feel her eyes on me as I walk away.

The party was already in full swing by the time

I made it home a little while ago. The marble countertops are littered with empty beer bottles, most of them imported or pricey craft brews. A few bottles of flavored vodka along with fruity mixers are on the island—Owen's attempt at being welcoming to the scantily-clad ladies scattered around the apartment—most of whom are perched in players' laps and draped over the sectional in the living room.

I probably sound like an old man at the ripe age of twenty-eight, but this is hardly fun anymore. Some nights I just want to go to bed…alone and in blissful peace and quiet. Yep, it's official, I need to apply for my AARP discounts and hand over my man card…stat.

Grabbing a six-pack of beer from the counter, I head into the living room. The guys are in rare form tonight. Winning the league championship will do that, I guess.

"Is that really Justin Brady?" a redhead asks from behind me as I head through the kitchen. I'm sure I look different without twenty pounds of hockey gear on, but the cynical side of me thinks about how inter-changeable the players are for girls like her. Bragging rights that you've bagged a pro player is practically the name of the game. Not that being someone's conquest has ever really bothered me before. But something about it annoys me as I weave my way through bodies.

Our star center, Asher, reaches out to bump his fist against mine as I walk past. "Awesome play tonight."

"Thanks, dude."

Someone hands me a shot as I pass and I down it without bothering to look what's in the glass.

Most of the team isn't just celebrating our win tonight. They're celebrating the fact that the off-season has just begun and a summer break of zero responsibilities is right around the corner.

Me? Not so much.

I eat, drink, and breathe hockey and so the idea of six weeks without the rigorous schedule to distract me is my own personal brand of hell.

I didn't have the easiest time growing up, and the breakdown of my family only made me play faster, fight harder, take more chances—and that's why we're winners celebrating tonight.

That said, when the two people who are supposed to love you unconditionally use you as nothing more than a pawn in their sick games, it warps your view on love. I wasn't lovable—I knew that.

I'd known that since I was six years old. And nothing had changed in the last twenty years. Women wanted me for my dick, and that was fine. That was really all I had to offer anyway.

I take up one half of the sofa, and work on polishing off my beer.

Teddy King, one of our best forwards and a total player, is making out with a girl in the corner.

"TK, get a fuckin' room!" someone calls out.

It's no surprise that Owen is on the couch with two blondes in his lap. He's my best friend, but the dude is a notorious player. "I hope you ladies are good at sharing," Owen says over the thumping music.

The blondes smile at each other, one of them turning to blink up at him. "And what will we be sharing?"

"My dick," he says, matter-of-factly.

The girls begin to giggle like he's just said the most interesting thing in the world.

I roll my eyes and open another beer from the six-pack at my feet.

Owen is six foot four and well over two hundred pounds of muscle with messy brown hair and the stubble of a beard he hasn't bothered to shave since we made the playoffs. He's one of the best goalies in the entire league, and he knows he's the shit. He's cocky, but he's earned the right to be. He plays it up well, and is known to be a total ladies' man. And the girls eat that shit up.

Normally I'd be doing the same exact thing, looking to blow off steam and celebrate our win, but tonight I can't seem to get out of my head long enough to relax. I'm more than a hard dick. I'm more than what I can do with a hockey stick. But most of these people here don't know that. Hell, I'm not even sure I know that anymore.

The only person here who looks to be as uneasy as me is Owen's younger sister, Elise. She's standing across the room, arms folded over her chest with her lips pressed into a firm line. The three of us grew up together a few hours from here in central Washington. I've known her since she was a bossy first-grader with a gap between her front teeth, and always wearing those shiny patent-leather shoes with frilly dresses.

Her looks, and her sense of fashion, have changed quite a bit. Her attitude, not so much. I can tell she's pissed about how out of hand things have gotten. I'm sure she'll be the first one here in the morning, nursing hangovers and helping us clean the apartment. There are at least fifty people here, and I know less than half of them.

A few seconds later, like she's heard my inner thoughts, Elise wanders closer and sits down next to me on the sofa. She looks so damn small in an oversized jersey and a pair of leggings. It's strange because most girls here are dressed in tiny black dresses that barely cover their asses and too much makeup, but Elise is nothing like that. Sometimes I forget she's all grown up, that she graduated from college last year, and is an actual adult.

"Hey, E." I raise my beer toward hers.

"Hey. Congrats on tonight."

"Thanks," I mutter after another long swig of beer. "You're not drinking?" I ask.

"I've had a couple," she says, her gaze still scanning the party, almost like she's making a concentrated effort not to look at me.

I know the feeling.

Normally—I see something I want—and I go and get it. It's how I've always been. It's how I'm wired. The one exception to that rule? Elise Parrish.

She's a no-fly zone. She used to be the cute kid sister of my best friend, but something shifted recently and I went from thinking of her as Owen's younger sister to something more.

This was the girl who borrowed my sweatshirts and never returned them. Took my warmest gloves and lost one somewhere between home and the ice rink. The girl who followed me and Owen around like a lost puppy all throughout our childhoods and the girl who cried during sappy commercials.

I had no idea how badly I would miss all those things about her until I moved away for college. But then my life got so busy with school and exams and hockey and fighting for a spot in the pros, my fascination with Elise took a backseat, and I knew it was for the best.

Still, despite my best efforts, she traipsed out of friend territory somewhere along the way, and into a sexy woman who made my dick ache. It was dangerous. And my best friend Owen made no apologies for the fact that his sister was very much off-limits to any member of our team.

My gaze drifts over to her again, and my breath catches. She's beautiful, intoxicatingly so. But she's smart too. And feisty. And she knows the game of hockey better than most of the guys, Lord knows she grew up spending just as much time at the ice rink as we did. Plus, the fact that I'm a pro hockey player doesn't impress her in the slightest. That's the best thing about her. I can just be myself.

"How pissed off are you?" I ask, unable to hide the amusement in my voice.

Elise shakes her head, the smirk on her mouth unmistakable. "On a scale of one to I'm going to murder Owen?"

"Sure." I polish off the rest of my beer and wait for her to answer, but she doesn't say anything else, she just lets out an exasperated sigh. So I grab another from the six-pack resting on the polished wood floor beneath my feet. "Want one?" I offer her a beer, but she shakes her head.

I drain half the bottle watching Asher and Teddy flirt with a group of girls on the balcony. They're eyeing the hot tub, which I'm suddenly sure will have floating remnants of jizz in the morning. Fucking fantastic.

"Those fuckers better not take those bunnies in the hot tub," Elise says under her breath.

I swallow a chuckle and shake my head.

"You're good peeps, E," I mumble, feeling the effects of the alcohol already.

Elise shakes her head, a smile tugging up her full lips. "I'm the freaking best. Someone's got to babysit this idiot team."

I study her for just a second. Long dark hair hanging over one shoulder, grey eyes that always seem to see straight through me, along with a sassy mouth that has always called me out on my bullshit.

But I never let myself notice things like that about her, and I won't start now, so I look down at the beer bottle in my hands instead.

When she's beside me, all my nerve endings light up with a feeling I can't explain.

I feel alive.

Raw.

On edge.

And there's no point in denying it—a whole lot turned on.

I need to get myself in check, but instead I'm feeling a little reckless. Unsteady.

"You know what will make this situation better?" I ask, sneaking one more glance at her.

"What's that?"

"Vodka."

Elise shakes her head.

"Come on, E-Class."

This earns me a laugh. The old nickname I bestowed on her in eighth grade still strikes a chord.

"I'll slice the lemons, you get the glasses?" she asks.

My heart starts to beat faster as she grins up at me. *Well damn, I didn't know I still had one of those.*

I smile back. "It's on."

• • •

*Get ready to meet your new favorite hot jocks in this series of stand-alone novels. If you like sexy, confident men who know how to handle a stick (on and off the ice), and smart women who are strong enough to keep all those big egos in check, this series of athlete romances is perfect for you!*

# Get Two Free books

Sign up for my newsletter and I'll automatically
send you two free books.

**www.kendallryanbooks.com/newsletter**

# Follow Kendall

BookBub has a feature where you can follow me and get an alert when I release a book or put a title on sale. Sign up here to stay in the loop:

www.bookbub.com/authors/kendall-ryan

*Website*

www.kendallryanbooks.com

*Facebook*

www.facebook.com/kendallryanbooks

*Twitter*

www.twitter.com/kendallryan1

*Instagram*

www.instagram.com/kendallryan1

*Newsletter*

www.kendallryanbooks.com/newsletter

# About the Author

A *New York Times*, *Wall Street Journal*, and *USA TODAY* bestselling author of more than two dozen titles, Kendall Ryan has sold over two million books, and her books have been translated into several languages in countries around the world. Her books have also appeared on the *New York Times* and *USA TODAY* bestseller list more than three dozen times. Kendall has been featured in publications such as *USA TODAY*, *Newsweek*, and *In Touch Magazine*. She lives in Texas with her husband and two sons.

To be notified of new releases or sales, join Kendall's private Mailing List.

**www.kendallryanbooks.com/newsletter**

Get even more of the inside scoop when you join Kendall's private Facebook group, Kendall's Kinky Cuties:

**www.facebook.com/groups/kendallskinkycuties**

# Other Books by Kendall Ryan

· *Unravel Me*
*Filthy Beautiful Lies Series*
*The Room Mate*
*The Play Mate*
*The House Mate*
*The Impact of You*
· *Screwed*
*The Fix Up*
*Dirty Little Secret*
*xo, Zach*
*Baby Daddy*
*Tempting Little Tease*
*Bro Code*
*Love Machine*
*Flirting with Forever*
*Dear Jane*
*Finding Alexei*
*Boyfriend for Hire*
*The Two Week Arrangement*

For a complete list of Kendall's books, visit:

**www.kendallryanbooks.com/all-books/**

CPSIA information can be obtained
at www.ICGtesting.com
Printed in the USA
BVHW031450020721
611053BV00008B/674

9 781673 648454